Matooke

by Tracy Turner-Jones and reminac kc

FRANKLIN WATTS
LONDON • SYDNEY

Eddie lived with his mama in a block of flats in the city. It was the school holidays and Eddie was going to stay with his auntie and cousin Susan in the countryside for the first time.

Eddie did not want to go to the countryside. He wanted to stay in the city and go skateboarding with his friends.

"Why can't I stay here?" he asked.

"I'm sorry, Eddie, but I have to work," Mama explained. "But you will like staying with Auntie. She will make you delicious matooke."

"I don't like matooke," Eddie said crossly.

Mama smiled. "You'll love Auntie's matooke."

To get to Auntie's house, they had to go on a big bus that went very slowly.

Then they had to ride on a boda-boda along a track that was very bumpy. "Look at all the monkeys!" Eddie shouted.

Auntie and cousin Susan were waiting outside their house. They hugged Mama and Eddie. Eddie was sad when it was time for Mama to go.

"I will be back soon," she promised.

Eddie, Auntie and Susan waved until they couldn't see Mama anymore.

Auntie made Eddie and Susan a warm cup of spicy chai. They sat on the porch to drink it.

"Now," said Auntie, "it's time to sweep up the leaves in the yard."
But Eddie really wanted to swing on the hammock.
"Come on," said Susan. "We have to sweep the leaves so we can put them in the basket."
So Eddie swept leaves with Auntie and Susan.

Soon there was a big pile of leaves.

"Now we have to put the leaves in the basket so we can take them to the plantation," Auntie said.

Eddie didn't want to pick up the leaves. He was worried he would get his new T-shirt dirty.

"Why do we have to go to the plantation?" Eddie asked.

"You'll see," said Auntie, with a grin.

Eddie grabbed some leaves and threw them into the basket.

Finally, the basket was full.

"You two carry the basket," Auntie said,

"and I will bring my rake in the wheelbarrow."

"When we get to the plantation, we can put

the leaves into the ground," Susan said.

"Didn't we just take the leaves **off** the ground?"

Eddie asked. But he wanted to help Auntie, so

he lifted the basket with Susan and off they

went.

9

On the plantation, there were lots of very tall matooke plants. As they walked between the plants, Eddie heard a rustling noise.

"Was that a snake?" he said.

"Are you scared of snakes?" Susan asked.

"No, of course not," Eddie said.

"Don't be afraid, Eddie. There aren't any snakes," Auntie said, laughing. "It's just a bird."

The ground in the plantation was all soft and spongy. Eddie wished he hadn't worn his favourite trainers.

At the end of the row of plants, Auntie's friend Frank was cutting down matooke. Frank told the children to tip the leaves onto the ground around the matooke plants.

"The leaves are good for the matooke," he said.

Auntie used her rake to push the leaves into the soil.

"We push the leaves into the ground to feed the trees," she told Eddie.

"Jump on the leaves with me, Eddie!" said Susan, laughing. "Then Frank can give us some matooke!"

Eddie didn't feel like jumping, so he stamped on the leaves very hard instead.

He stamped faster and faster. Susan jumped and Eddie stamped. He liked stamping. It was fun!

"Thank you for bringing the leaves for the trees," Frank said. "Now you can choose a bunch of matooke to take home for your dinner." Auntie took some matooke and put it in the wheelbarrow. Eddie helped push the wheelbarrow back to Auntie's house.

"And now," said Auntie, "It is time to cook the matooke."
Eddie followed Auntie and Susan into their kitchen.
"Erm ... Auntie?" he said. "I don't really like matooke."
"You'll love my matooke," Auntie said, grinning.

She made a fire under a big pot.

Then she peeled the matooke and ground up the spices. The children chopped the vegetables and put them into the pot. Eddie liked stirring as the vegetables sizzled.

"Thank you," said Auntie. "Now you can go and play while the matooke cooks."

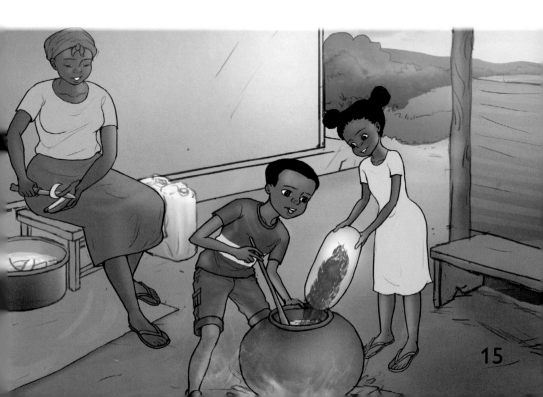

15

A little bit later, Eddie smelled something

very sweet and spicy.

"Dinner time," Auntie called.

"Eddie told me he doesn't want any,"

Susan said.

But the wonderful smell made

Eddie's mouth water.

"Well, I **am** hungry," he said. "I will try

a little bite."

Eddie tried a bit of the food on his plate.

Then he tried a bit more. Then he ate it all up.

 "**That** was matooke?" he asked.

"Yes!" Auntie and Susan said together.

Suddenly Eddie pushed back his chair and ran to get a broom.

"What are you doing?" asked Auntie.

Eddie smiled. "I'm going to sweep up more leaves," he said.

"Why?" asked Susan.

"So I can take the leaves to the plantation and give them to the trees," Eddie replied. "Then when Mama comes, we can have some more matooke."

"But you don't like matooke," said Auntie and Susan, laughing.

"Yes, I do!" said Eddie, smiling.

"I **love** matooke!"

Story order

Look at these 5 pictures and captions.
Put the pictures in the right order
to retell the story.

1

Eddie stamps on the leaves.

2

They prepare matooke together.

3

Eddie and Mum travel to the countryside.

4

Eddie loves matooke!

5

They rake up the leaves.

Independent Reading

This series is designed to provide an opportunity for your child to read on their own. These notes are written for you to help your child choose a book and to read it independently.

In school, your child's teacher will often be using reading books which have been banded to support the process of learning to read. Use the book band colour your child is reading in school to help you make a good choice. *Matooke* is a good choice for children reading at White Band in their classroom to read independently.

The aim of independent reading is to read this book with ease, so that your child enjoys the story and relates it to their own experiences.

About the book

Eddie is a city boy from Kampala, but he's off for a visit with his auntie and cousin in the Ugandan countryside. It's hard for him to get used to it at first. In the end, Auntie's delicious matooke wins him over.

Before reading

Help your child to learn how to make good choices by asking: "Why did you choose this book? Why do you think you will enjoy it?" Ask your child about what they know about fruit plantations (or farms). Then look at the cover with your child and ask: "Where do you think this story is set?"

Remind your child that they can break words into groups of syllables or sound out letters to make a word if they get stuck.

Decide together whether your child will read the story independently or read it aloud to you.

During reading

Remind your child of what they know and what they can do independently. If reading aloud, support your child if they hesitate or ask for help by telling the word. If reading to themselves, remind your child that they can come and ask for your help if stuck.

After reading

Support comprehension by asking your child to tell you about the story. Use the story order puzzle to encourage your child to retell the story in the right sequence, in their own words. The correct sequence can be found on the next page.

Help your child think about the messages in the book that go beyond the story and ask: "What lessons did Eddie learn during his time with his cousin and auntie? How did his attitude change over the course of the story?"

Give your child a chance to respond to the story: "What was your favourite part of the book? Why?"

Extending learning

Help your child predict other possible outcomes of the story by asking: "What if Eddie hadn't been brave and tried the matooke? How would he and his cousin and auntie be feeling at the end?"

In the classroom, your child's teacher may be teaching predicting what might happen on the basis of what has been read so far. Ask your child to find some clues in the story that indicate why they are tidying leaves and taking them to a plantation. Ask them to look for clues about Eddie's attitude throughout, too. Considering how Eddie behaved, did they expect him to try the matooke and love it? Look at the plot and key events and ask them to pinpoint two or three events that are important and how each one affects what happens next, to reinforce story sequencing.

Franklin Watts
First published in Great Britain in 2020
by The Watts Publishing Group

Copyright © The Watts Publishing Group 2020
All rights reserved.

Series Editors: Jackie Hamley and Melanie Palmer and Grace Glendinning
Series Advisors: Dr Sue Bodman and Glen Franklin
Series Designers: Peter Scoulding and Cathryn Gilbert

A CIP catalogue record for this book is
available from the British Library.

ISBN 978 1 4451 7219 4 (hbk)
ISBN 978 1 4451 7220 0 (pbk)
ISBN 978 1 4451 7232 3 (library ebook)
ISBN 978 1 4451 7921 6 (ebook)

Printed in China

Franklin Watts
An imprint of
Hachette Children's Group
Part of The Watts Publishing Group
Carmelite House
50 Victoria Embankment
London EC4Y 0DZ

An Hachette UK Company
www.hachette.co.uk

www.reading-champion.co.uk

Answer to Story order: 3, 5, 1, 2, 4